Just Bite Me: A Guide to Zombies, Vampires, Werewolves, and Other Walking Nightmares

Marc Hoover

Edited by Sigrid Macdonald
http://www.bookmagic.ca/

ISBN: 0692691995
ISBN 13: 9780692691991
Library of Congress Control Number: 2016939002
Wise Grandpa Books, Batavia, OH

TABLE OF CONTENTS

INTRODUCTION

Every crop of horror fans has its own definition of a monster. Horror fans born in the 1950s considered *The Blob* terrifying. If you haven't seen this classic, it's worth seeing. Imagine a dish of gelatin trying to devour you for lunch. Sure it's hokey, but viewers in the 1950s loved it.

Millennial horror fans might find vampires wearing makeup and tight jeans terrifying. For this, we can thank Stephanie Meyer for introducing us to lovesick teenage werewolves and vampires. In her *Twilight* series, she created a vivid love story involving Bella, a teenage girl who falls in love with Edward, a vampire doomed to remain a teenager forever.

For anyone on the downside of forty, never ask a teenager to watch a classic horror movie with you. They will laugh at the comical special effects and corny plots. If you watch one of these with a child or grandchild, they will ask how such a cheesy movie could scare anyone.

Modern horror fans share a common love for brain-hungry zombies. The American Movie Channel (AMC) has the most popular television series in cable history—a program called *The Walking Dead*. America has a love affair with walking, flesh-eating corpses. The graphic novels depict a sheriff, his family, and other survivors, struggling to avoid losing their brains and limbs to hungry zombies.

Why do zombies, vampires, and other repulsive creatures terrify us? Why are we so drawn to creatures with putrid flesh, nasty teeth, and oozing bodily fluids? We love our monsters because we know they don't exist—or do they? Do a Google search on monsters, and you will find more pages than you could read in a lifetime or two if you happen to be a ghoul or a vampire.

According to a 2011 MSN.com article, the zombie industry generates $5 billion annually. Visit any Wal-Mart or Target, and you will find video games, comics, and zombie movies. The zombie business is prosperous and doesn't show any signs of slowing down. Americans are fascinated with any urban legend involving the paranormal.

Bobby Mackey's Music World in Wilder, Kentucky, is America's most haunted nightclub. Ghost hunters from around the globe have descended on his club searching for paranormal activity. Ghost hunters have reported many strange events. Bobby Mackey's is allegedly haunted by Pearl Bryan, an Indiana woman who was beheaded by her lover. Countless people have witnessed paranormal activity in the club.

Have you ever wondered if werewolves or vampires exist? If none of these monsters ever existed, why have their legends survived for so many centuries? This book is an unofficial guide to zombies, mummies, vampires, and other famous monsters. You will need to decide for yourself whether any of these legends are true or if they are only fairy tales.

I cannot guarantee you won't see a gremlin on your next flight or a vampire needing blood. However, after reading this book, you will know the difference between a zombie and a werewolf. Several monster legends I discuss date back many centuries ago. Since it's impossible to trace the roots of these monsters to one source, I focus on the most popular myths. Now it's time to meet your favorite walking nightmares!

1

ZOMBIES

The sun is blinding and shares its warm rays with anyone who can appreciate its warmth. It's a time for family vacations, grilling out, swimming, and romance. Couples are visiting local parks, holding hands, and sharing embraces. The dog walkers and elderly also enjoy frequenting local parks. But only a few miles away, turbulence is stirring in the local boneyard.

Silent chants float through the air.

A chilling breeze silently whispers, *Brains! Brains! Brains!* The chant becomes one with the old boneyard and caresses the remains of its residents. The remains are rotten and long forgotten.

Madness soon rises from underneath crusty ground. Dirt covered phalanges protrude through unholy mounds of earth. Prodding fingers still wear wedding rings, necklaces, and other reminders of a former life. Other fingers clutch handfuls of dirt clumps encased with shreds of grass.

Skeletal arms puncture the soft dirt and raise their arms in protest. These dead creatures once held jobs, wrote poetry, and held loved ones in what they used to call arms. Now, the dead fingers writhe and clutch dirt and shards of their rotting coffins. The living don't hear the cracking phalanges and metacarpal bones. These creatures now seek sustenance.

Zombie skulls resemble burned out Jack-O-lanterns. The skulls no longer contain eyeballs or flesh. The worms have taken residence, and the dead have returned to devour the living.

With tattered flesh dangling from bones like wind chimes, the dead silently infiltrate the surrounding subdivisions. Ragged burial clothing wrap long-dead skeletons like a bandage. These horrors do not speak or dance. They only exist to collect their pound of flesh. They will soon feast on blood, brains, and pale fleshy skin. The zombies are on the march.

Before 1968, zombies weren't flesh-eating monsters. Director George Romero introduced flesh-eating zombies in a movie titled *Night of the Living Dead.* After Hell closed its doors, evil had nowhere to go. Their only recourse was to kill the living and inherit the planet.

Before Romero, zombies preferred to wash clothing or pick crops. The zombie legend originates from Haiti, where bokors converted locals into mindless slaves. Bokors are similar to witch doctors. They used Voodoo spells, chants, and superstition to keep locals in fear. Before George Romero, zombies weren't known for craving brains.

Zombies are lifeless creatures that live on instinct. They still have memories of their former lives. They just cannot make a connection. They must roam the Earth until someone destroys them. Many horror fans are comparable to zombies. Although they love gore, they don't know why. True horror fans will enjoy any movie with a monster. Often, a rotten horror movie with horrific acting won't deter a true horror fan from watching it.

Most zombie movie fans recognize the George Romero zombie: a dead creature with rotting flesh and a rancid odor. The creature seeks tasty brains from the living. Zombies are former parents, friends, or lovers. Not only will they invite you to dinner, but they will make you the main course. The Hollywood zombie is the flesh-eating monster we know, love, and fear.

Interesting enough, no one on *The Walking Dead* refers to the undead as zombies. Rick Grimes and his people refer to them as either "biters" or "walkers." In Hollywood, the zombie tag has been misapplied to a hybrid between a vampire and a ghoul. A ghoul is an evil beast that robs graves and feeds on corpses.

A vampire is a blood drinking, nocturnal creature. If a ghoul and a vampire procreated, you might have a bloodthirsty creature that enjoys biting people. For entertainment purposes, it's easier just to call this creature a zombie. So if a zombie isn't a blood sucking walking corpse, what is it?

Based on Haitian folklore, a zombie isn't dead. The Haitian word for a zombie is "zombi," which means the spirit of the dead. The zombie legend originated from Voodoo practicing Haitians. Today, Haitians still practice Voodoo.

Also, Haiti zombies did not eat people. Instead, zombies became mindless servants who served the bokors. A bokor creates a poison from Tetrodoxin, a powerful toxin found inside a Puffer fish. After the victim eats the toxin, he becomes comatose.

The victim's heartbeat slows until he appears dead. The victim is buried alive and later dug up by the bokor. The victim then lives to serve the bokor, who converts his victims into mindless laborers. In Haitian culture, zombies still exist. Early zombie movies followed the Haitian theme. They had only fallen under the control of an evil fiend. In 1932, a film titled *White Zombie* followed the Haitian zombie legend. Madeleine, the lead heroine, was poisoned and became a zombie. She found herself under the control of Murder Legendre, an evil madman portrayed by actor Bela Lugosi.

By today's standards, horror fans consider *The White Zombie* tame. Haitians believe a zombie can be returned to humanity if he eats salt or visits the ocean. Allegedly, a bokor can bring the dead back to life and convert the deceased into a zombie after the soul departs.

Sorry to disappoint true zombie fans, but a real zombie is more likely to be hacking away at a sugarcane crop instead of eating your brain. However, today's monster movie fans aren't going to shell out cash to watch a zombie do manual labor. In the original zombie movies, we feared the living more than the dead. Today's monster fan demands brain eating zombies.

So why do we fear zombies? Because they force us to face our mortality. Zombies represent death—something no one avoids. As we age, we realize that we already have one foot standing in the grave. This terrifies us because we do not know what happens to us after we die. We cannot accept that our bodies will one day rot away underneath a mound of dirt. Although dying is natural, death is still difficult to accept. Zombies give credence to our fears of the unknown.

2

THE ZOMBIE APOCALYPSE

The idea of a zombie apocalypse is far-fetched, but it has become a trendy topic among today's youth. George Romero created the zombie apocalypse culture with his movies. *Night of the Living Dead* and *Dawn of the Dead* depict what can happen during a hostile zombie takeover.

One of the characters in *Dawn of the Dead* explained why zombies existed. "When there's no more room in Hell, the dead will walk the Earth." The zombie apocalypse is the final judgment of man: a day when men will pay for the transgressions they have committed against the land, wildlife, and our natural resources.

It's a day of reckoning when chemicals and nuclear waste ravage the masses. Even the Centers for Disease Control and Prevention website (www.cdc.gov) offers a plan for the zombie apocalypse. But don't assume the government will pass out guns and machetes to every wannabe zombie killer. It's a survival plan for anyone still alive when the country goes to Hell. Spinning doomsday tales are nothing new.

Before Romero, Mary Shelley wrote *The Last Man* in 1826. The novel portrays a group of people who try to survive a killer plague. Shelley also wrote *Frankenstein*.

In *One Second After*, William Forstchen wrote a compelling tale involving an unknown enemy that destroys America without firing a shot. Instead of using firearms, unknown terrorists sever mankind's dependence on technology. After losing the use of computers, cars, and phones, an unseen enemy watches America destroy itself. Afterward, a new primitive world evolves. Within months, Americans become savage primitives who turn to murder and cannibalism.

The Bible's book of Revelations describes war, famine, and pestilence as the apocalypse. The Bible has existed for at least 1,000 years forever and explains the final days of man. George Romero just added zombies and made it scarier.

3

CLASSIC HORROR MOVIES

Horror stories are a billion dollar industry with millions of devoted fans. Although Stephanie Meyer's *Twilight* series isn't considered over-the-top horrific, it does involve werewolves and blood-lusting vampires. It appealed to audiences worldwide and earned more than $100 million.

Before Twilight, horror fans embraced Jason Voorhees, Michael Myers, and Freddie Krueger—three monster superstars from *Friday the 13th*, *Halloween*, and *Nightmare on Elm Street*. Bela Lugosi, Boris Karloff, Peter Cushing, Vincent Price, and Christopher Lee appeared in Hollywood's earliest classics.

Horror movies have come a long way from the silent black and white films. In 1922, Max Schreck acted in *Nosferatu*, a silent film featuring the evil Dr. Orlok, a balding, rat-faced vampire. Today's horror movies barely resemble their ancestors.

Classic favorites like *I Was a Teenage Werewolf* and *The Blob* wouldn't appeal to current horror movie fans. Special effects have become so advanced that moviemakers may eventually discontinue using real actors in horror movies.

Instead of using fake blood and gore, computer animators can generate lifelike monsters that will appeal to future horror movie buffs. Today's movie studios can take a book like *World War Z* and turn it into a blockbuster movie capable of grossing more than $200,000,000. The horror industry is valuable, if not crucial, to our economy because the industry creates careers, tax revenues, and entertainment. It has become a culture in American society.

4

UFOS

The unidentified flying object (UFO) is an unknown spacecraft or any other unexplained object seen flying in the sky. For centuries, people have reported UFO sightings from all over the world. Early reports date back to China during the fourth century. However, when it comes to aliens, most people refer to one of the strangest incidents in American history: an event still discussed more than sixty years later!

In 1947, a strange object fell from the sky and landed on a ranch near Roswell, New Mexico. The ranch foreperson investigated the debris and notified the sheriff, who then contacted military authorities at Roswell Army Air Field. Intelligence officer Major Jesse Marcel recovered debris from the crash site and found tinfoil, wooden sticks, rubber, and metallic I-beams. He even posed for a photograph with a substance that resembled the same tinfoil you might use to cover leftover food.

On July 8, 1947, the military announced Major Marcel had found a weather balloon: the remnants of Project Mogul, a program once used to detect Soviet nuclear tests. The public didn't accept the explanation. People suspected something more sinister than a weather balloon. Once conspiracy theorists discovered this story, whispers flooded the desert with tales of recovered dead aliens. The Air Force responded to this theory—the alleged aliens were recovered crash test dummies. Roswell continues to remain a tourist attraction and the world's UFO mecca.

Invasion of the Flying Saucers

In 1948, Kenneth Arnold, an amateur pilot, reported seeing nine crescent-shaped objects flying around Mount Rainier in Washington. He referred to the strange objects as "saucers skipping on water." A local newspaper misquoted Arnold by saying the objects resembled saucers. After more than sixty years, we still refer to strange alien ships as flying saucers. UFOs have become so popular that Tinsel Town stars and political leaders have reported visions of mysterious flying aircraft.

U.S. Representative Dennis Kucinich said he and actress Shirley MacLaine once witnessed a UFO. Even former President Jimmy Carter claims he saw a UFO in Georgia. Then you have *Ghostbuster* actor Dan Aykroyd's unusual take on aliens. He claims aliens travel back and forth to Earth like taxis. If true, he didn't mention how to hail one.

The Government Looks to the Stars for Aliens

After the Roswell and Kenneth Arnold incidents, the U.S. military began to explore possible alien life. In 1948, the government developed a series of projects concentrated on extraterrestrial life. After Project Sign (1948) and Project Grudge (1952), the military compiled more than 12,000 UFO reports for Project Blue Book (1952-1969). The program operated from Wright-Patterson Air Force Base in Dayton, Ohio. Although the military identified most of the cases, a small percentage remained unidentified. After a decrease in sightings, the military abandoned Project Blue Book in 1969.

Alien Abductions

For years, people have claimed that aliens have abducted them. These individuals say that strange creatures with enormous eyeballs captured and probed them. Hollywood has even made movies about alleged alien abductions.

Ask anyone if they believe in flying spaceships and little green aliens and you will find a divided camp. Others believe the universe is so vast that it is unreal to conclude we are the only living beings in the universe. Are we alone? This question will continue to be asked until we meet a real alien.

5

GHOSTS/HAUNTED HOUSES

From the LaLaurie House in French Quarters, Louisiana, to Bobby Mackey's Music World in Northern Kentucky, some people think these places still shelter the dead. The general belief is when people die under tragic circumstances, their spirits continue to linger. Maybe they still seek justice or loved life too much to leave.

The Internet and the local library provide excellent resources for finding local haunted houses. Unless someone personally witnesses paranormal activity, he or she may not believe in ghosts. Douglas Hensley wrote *Hell's Gate: Terror at Bobby Mackey's Music World*. He delves into the building's history of murder and intrigue. To this day, Kentuckians say that Pearl Bryan's restless spirit haunts Bobby Mackey's. Allegedly, in 1896, Scott Jackson and Alonzo Walling murdered and beheaded Bryan somewhere on the property. But others believe the crime happened elsewhere. Supposedly, Jackson murdered Bryan because she became pregnant with a child he didn't want.

In 1897, authorities hanged Jackson and Walling for their heinous crime. Local police officers and other patrons have signed sworn statements about paranormal activity surrounding the club. Ghost hunters and psychics have concluded that dead people still enjoy listening to music at Bobby Mackey's place.

Another house with a troubled past is the former LaLaurie mansion in New Orleans. Troy Taylor describes the horrific tale in *The Haunted New Orleans*. It involves the most famous ghost story in the French Quarter: the oldest neighborhood in New Orleans. In 1832, Dr. Louis LaLaurie, his wife Delphine, and two of her daughters from previous marriages lived in a three-story mansion built at 1140 Royal Street in the French Quarter.

The mansion once had enormous chandeliers and European dishes. Locals knew the LaLaurie's for their wealth, fashionable clothing, and fabulous parties. Madame LaLaurie became the most influential and stunning woman in New Orleans. However, her splendor and wealth masked a cruel and immoral woman.

Today, she could easily hold court with serial killers Ted Bundy, John Wayne Gacy, Aileen Wuornos, and Richard Ramirez. Madame LaLaurie, a deranged woman, experienced sheer pleasure in torturing and murdering her victims. During the early 1830s, Louisiana law recognized slavery as legal; but the law restricted slave owners from abusing their slaves.

Although she showered her houseguests and friends with love and attention, she despised her slaves. She considered them lower than animals. Ultimately, neighbors began noticing and whispering about how the LaLaurie slaves just vanished. Neighbors concluded that something strange was happening inside the mansion.

One day, a neighbor witnessed Madame LaLaurie chasing a slave girl with a whip. The frightened child escaped LaLaurie's wrath by leaping to her death. The young girl was buried underneath a tree on the property. A neighbor reported the act, which violated laws forbidding cruel treatment of slaves. Authorities confiscated the slaves and sold them off to other slave owners. Madame LaLaurie then convinced friends and relatives to buy the slaves.

She then bought them back and returned them to her mansion of horrors. The abuse incident left her a pariah. Friends soon distanced themselves from the LaLaurie family. In 1834, a fire exposed the whispered secrets kept hidden within the LaLaurie mansion walls.

A 70-year-old cook, chained to a stove by her ankle, had set the mansion on fire in a suicide attempt.

Firefighters soon made a horrific discovery. Behind a hidden door in the attic, they found slaves chained to a wall and strapped to tables. They also witnessed a slave locked inside an animal cage. It seemed that someone had created a torture chamber. *The New Orleans Bee* reported the victims were stripped naked and abused. Women had their stomachs cut open while the men had their eyes removed and severed genitals. Authorities also found a man with a hole in his head and a stick inside the hole used to stir the man's brain. Authorities and locals believed that Dr. LaLaurie knew about his wife's evil deeds but had ignored them.

After the appalling discovery, an angry mob stormed the mansion with hanging ropes. The LaLaurie family escaped mob justice with their necks still intact. No one ever saw them again. Speculation is that family members hid them.

Since then, people have reported ghostly sightings of former slaves and still hear agonizing cries of distress coming from tortured souls who once suffered at 1140 Royal Street. Other reports include someone who claimed to have been attacked by a ghostly black man in chains. Future entrepreneurs transformed the abandoned building into a rental property, a saloon, and then a furniture store.

Regardless, no one has ever stayed in the old house for long. The former furniture store owner claimed someone had vandalized his property. The angry owner stayed overnight to catch the vandals. By dawn, someone or something had damaged the furniture and covered it in a strange slime. The owner closed his business after realizing nothing human could have caused such havoc.

The secrets of torture and murder will remain inside the old mansion forever. As of this writing, the former LaLaurie mansion still exists. Whether you believe in haunted houses or not, people have told ghost stories around campfires for centuries.

6

GHOULS

Ghouls first appeared in a collection of Arabic stories titled *One Thousand and One Nights*. Various authors wrote the stories during the Islamic Golden Age. In one story, a prince named Gherib battles a family of ghouls and then converts them to Islam. The ghoul is a mystical Arabic creature that originated from the Arabic words "ghul" or "ghulah."

According to Arabic legend, a ghoul is an evil demon that drinks blood and eats corpses. After feasting on its victim, a ghoul can assume the victim's shape. The flesh-eating ghoul has an insatiable hunger and hides in graveyards and other isolated locations.

A female ghoul is more cunning than the male because she doesn't kill her victims instantly. She uses deception to capture and marry an unsuspecting human man. The marriage won't last though because she will devour her unsuspecting husband's flesh. During the 19th century, superstitious people feared anything without an explanation. These superstitions led people to believe in disappearing corpses. Although illogical, people had good reason to believe that something was removing corpses from their graves. Imagine visiting a relative after his funeral. Nothing remains other than a hole in the ground.

Rumors spread that something was robbing graves and devouring corpses—and this is how the ghoul legend eerily crept into Western Civilization.

Soon, superstition and fear began keeping locals away from graveyards. If a ghoul could devour a corpse, what could it do to someone who is alive? Fear soon created the perfect cover for ghouls to complete their despicable work under darkness.

Advances in 19th century medicine led to a problem worse than ghouls. Medical schools had trouble acquiring enough cadavers for their students. Apparently, people weren't charitable about donating their bodies to a medical school—and without experimenting on cadavers, medical students couldn't become doctors.

A shortage of cadavers created a black market for grave robbers willing to dig up corpses for profit. After grave diggers had unearthed the bodies, medical schools purchased them without any questions asked.

Although most grave robbers waited for someone to die, others murdered their victims. In the 1820s, William Burke and William Hare formed a gruesome partnership and killed at least fifteen victims. Afterward, they sold their victims to Professor Robert Knox of the Edinburgh Medical School.

Authorities soon uncovered the grisly murders and arrested the killers. Hare then turned snitch and testified against Burke. A court convicted Burke and executed him in January of 1829. Hare changed his name and left town.

7

TROLLS

A troll is an evil monster with a Scandinavian history. Trolls are described as vile, ugly, and lacking intelligence. However, brains aren't necessary for any creature that stands more than ten-feet tall and can easily remove your head with his enormous hands. The troll has a tough, stone-like skin and can regenerate its body. Only fire or sunlight can kill a troll.

A children's Norwegian fairy tale titled *The Three Billy Goats Gruff* involved an ugly troll and three goats trying to cross a bridge. Unknown to the brothers, a hungry troll lurked underneath the bridge. The smallest goat tried to cross first. He convinced the stupid troll to allow him to cross and wait for his middle brother. The troll spared the little goat and waited for the middle goat. When the middle brother tried to cross the bridge, he convinced the troll to wait for his oldest brother, who was the largest of the three goats.

Finally, the oldest brother arrived. The ugly troll told the oldest goat that he shall feast on his flesh, but the oldest Gruff wasn't planning on becoming anyone's dinner. He attacked the troll, poked out his eyes, and kicked him off the bridge. This short tale proves trolls aren't too bright. Otherwise, he would have eaten the younger siblings and avoided the largest brother.

Like other monsters, troll history also varies based on the storyteller. The average troll can regenerate itself, but every legend has its exceptions. For instance, not all trolls fear sunlight. Some may disapprove of it, but they can still hunt in daylight.

Trolls also aren't too picky about what's on the menu. They will devour wood, metal, horses, and the occasional human. Like people, a troll may also have a preference as to where it sleeps. They live in caves, mountains, swamps, and underneath bridges. The ones underneath bridges enjoy waiting for an unsuspecting traveler and then attacking and eating him.

Oddly, female trolls aren't as brutal and prefer the company of mortal men. Writer Robert Lamb of the How Stuff Works website wrote the following: "The female troll may appear as beautiful women as a means of attracting male humans, which their horrible menfolk then brutalize." Trolls are creatures you do not ever want to meet. They are unpredictable, powerful, and difficult to kill.

8

GOBLINS

Based on whatever dark and dank place they call home, a goblin's itinerary depends on wherever it lives. The J.R.R. Tolkien's Lord of the Ring's version roamed Middle Earth and had ties to another disgusting Middle Earth creature called an Orc. Tolkien's goblins were half the size of a man and carried swords and spears. Goblins are vile creatures known for having an obsession with gold.

Another goblin-type-creature with German roots is a kobold, which is often considered a goblin, according to several websites and books. Others disagree and think kobolds are closer to gnomes, fairies, brownies, and less likely to be goblins.

In 1973, Hollywood unleashed a terrifying thriller titled *Don't Be Afraid of the Dark*. The original version kept many children from sleeping without a night light on—myself included. The movie focused on a goblin myth involving dark magic. Evidently, goblins kidnap women and children and then use their magical powers to transform their victims into goblins.

The only way to stop them is to keep the lights on because they fear the light, which explains why they find solace in the darkness of their victim's home. Then you have a celebrity goblin known for shaking down mobsters, committing crimes, and killing anyone who interferes in his business dealings.

This famous goblin is the Green Goblin, a Marvel Comics villain. He is Spiderman's most deadly nemesis because he knows Spiderman's secret identity. The Green Goblin is Norman Osborne, a respected businessman who lost his sanity after surviving an explosion. Regardless of origin, goblins share one identical feature—they love trouble.

9

DRAGONS

The word dragon has a Greek origin, translated from the word Draconta, which means to watch. Dragons are obsessed with hoarding gold. They may have wings, horns, a long tail, and a hunger for death and destruction.

One well-known dragon is Smog, a hostile, fire-breathing dragon created by J.R.R. Tolkien in his fantasy book titled *The Hobbit*. Although no one knows who created the dragon legend, some scholars believe a correlation exists between dragons and dinosaur bones.

In past centuries, people may not have known the difference between a Tyrannosaurus Rex and a fire-breathing dragon, but thanks to advances in science, many people have seen dinosaur fossils on television and in museums. Our ancestors probably didn't make the connection between dragons and dinosaurs as we have. They may have concluded that massive dinosaur bones must have been the remains of a dragon.

Dragons live in mountains, caves, volcanoes or even in the ocean. While some breathe fire, others breathe acid, poison, and lightning. The Draconika.com website describes five different dragons:

Black Dragons: An evil carnivorous dragon that breathes acid and prefers to ambush its prey. This nocturnal killer survives by eating fish, eels, and an occasional human. Black dragons live in swamps and thrive in putrid environments.

Red Dragons: Another evil dragon that devours flesh. The Red Dragon is a greedy gold hoarder. Red dragons live in mountains, volcanoes, or in warm climates. A Red Dragon has a forked tongue, wings, breathes fire, and enjoys eating human flesh and drinking human blood.

Blue Dragons: A vain dragon with a horn on its head that breathes lightning. A Blue Dragon lives in a dry region similar to a desert. It feasts on camels, lizards, and other desert creatures.

Green Dragons: An intelligent and cruel dragon that is carnivorous and lives in the forest. The Green Dragon is a predator and enjoys hunting its prey. Green dragons also breathe a toxic chlorine gas and resemble the long-necked Brontosaurus.

White Dragons: The White Dragon is smaller than other dragons and lives in the Arctic. This loner avoids hunting and feasts on animals that have died from the cold. It breathes an icy frost and may retreat if attacked.

During the Middle Ages, churches associated dragons with Satan. For instance, one famous dragon story with a religious overtone involved St. George—a knight who slayed a dragon and rescued a fair maiden. Saint George protected himself with a cross and became a Christian after killing the dragon. Scholars also believed in a connection between fire-breathing dragons and the fiery pits of Hell.

Today, dragons are still popular. They appear in video games, novels, music, cartoons, and movies. Although, dragons almost always portray the evil villains, some aren't evil. For instance, in 1963, the group Peter, Paul and Mary released a classic song about a friendly dragon titled *Puff the Magic Dragon*. In 1977,

Disney released a movie called *Pete's Dragon* about an orphan who befriends an invisible dragon. So whether people are singing or dreaming about imaginary dragons, they remain one of the world's oldest legends.

10

THE MUMMY

In 1922, an English archeologist named Howard Carter discovered King Tutankhamun's (King Tut) burial ground. According to a *National Geographic* article about King Tut, he stood 5' 6" and died around nineteen. He had excellent health and no cavities.

A mummy wasn't anything more than a well-preserved Pharaoh wrapped in strips of linen cloth. A linen wrapped preserved Pharaoh wasn't too terrifying until someone from the media attached a curse to King Tutankhamun's sacred burial ground.

In 1923, Lord Carnarvon, who financed Carter's mission, died under suspicious circumstances. The King Tut One website (www.kingtutone.com) claims that Lord Carnarvon became ill and died from a mosquito bite. The media released stories that King Tut had reached from beyond the grave to unleash the deadly curse that killed Lord Carnarvon.

Nevertheless, someone forgot to include Howard Carter in on the curse since he lived to be sixty-four. Detractors referenced Carter's life to dispel the curse. If it existed, why didn't Carter die sooner? Logical reasoning supports King Tut cursing Carter since he dug up King Tut's tomb and not Lord Carnarvon, who only funded the project.

The King Tut curse led to the latest monster creation. By combining a mummified Pharaoh and a curse, moviemakers created a mummy that returns to destroy anyone who dared to keep him from getting a good night's sleep.

In 1932, Boris Karloff starred in the movie *The Mummy*. He portrayed Imhotep, a high priest who returned from the dead after nearly 4,000 years. Imhotep then took his revenge by killing and maiming the English archeologists who disturbed his eternal sleep. He kidnapped a woman he believed to be his reincarnated lady love from 4,000 years ago.

In 1999, Imhotep once again returned to the big screen in a movie also called *The Mummy*. Actor Brendan Frasier appeared as the latest hero to fight the evil Imhotep. The movie used the latest special effects and computer graphics to revive Imhotep. Although the mummy isn't Hollywood's most terrifying monster, we should still recognize him as extraordinary.

11

GODZILLA

Godzilla (a.k.a. Gojira) made his debut in 1954 and has become the most famous monster in Japanese history. Although he doesn't drink blood or survive on human flesh, he can destroy entire cities and cause massive death and destruction. Toho, the Japanese movie studio, has turned Godzilla into an international superstar that has appeared in movies, comics, toys, cartoons, and video games. The Godzilla Wikia website offers insight on Godzilla's true origin.

Gojira is a Japanese word that combines Gorira (gorilla) and Kujira (whale). The words combine Godzilla's ability to thrive in the water like a whale and an ability to fight with the brutal strength of a gorilla. Toho settled on using Godzilla as the proper English translation from Gojira.

In the first Godzilla movie, *Godzilla*, Doctor Daisuke Serizawa destroyed Godzilla with an oxygen weapon that disintegrates Godzilla. Doctor Serizawa also died in the conflict. Knowing Godzilla's true origin is difficult. Different movies have offered several conflicting opinions. For instance, in *King Kong vs. Godzilla*, a scientist says Godzilla is a combination of the Tyrannosaurus Rex and the Stegosaurus.

In another movie, Godzilla is classified as a dinosaur known as the "Godzillasaurus." After this dinosaur became exposed to radiation from nuclear weapons testing, he grew to be 50 meters tall and weighed 20,000 tons. Another theory is that radiation from the nuclear bombs used on Hiroshima and Nagasaki during WWII mutated a reptile into Godzilla. After battles against King Kong, Mothra, Monster X, and Megalon, Godzilla has continued his reign as "King of the Monsters."

12

KING KONG

Filmmaker Merian Caldwell Cooper created and released *King Kong* in 1933. The movie featured heroine Ann Darrow (Fay Wray), movie director Carl Denham (Robert Armstrong), and First Mate Jack Driscoll (Bruce Cabot), but King Kong, also known as the eighth wonder of the world, was the star. Hollywood has tried to recapture Kong's magic with remakes in 1976 and 2005.

Although the three movies had their technological differences and plot variations, both remakes followed the original theme—a beast falls hard for a beautiful woman. Ann Darrow was the one dame who had hooked Kong with her blonde locks and smooth skin.

The 1933 movie began with Carl Denham, a director known for making exotic animal movies. Afterwards, he convinced an unemployed woman named Ann Darrow to star in his next movie. Once Denham secured a crew and an actress, he set sail to find a location. What he didn't tell anyone was that he wanted to film on an undiscovered island never seen by civilized eyes. Denham only told the secret mission to Jack Driscoll.

Denham had heard rumors about a mysterious island inhabited by natives and a creature named Kong. Denham committed to finding out more about this unknown creature. Denham, Driscoll, and the Venture crew arrived on a mysterious island called Skull Island—an uncharted island without electricity, indoor plumbing, and civilized people. An enormous ape named Kong ruled the island. He shared the reclusive island with natives and dinosaurs. The natives worshiped Kong and appeased him with female sacrifices.

Once Denham arrived on Skull Island, he organized a scouting party to investigate the island. Ann Darrow also joined the group. While exploring the island, the crew discovered the island's native inhabitants. In awe of Darrow's beauty, the native chief offered to trade six of his women for Darrow.

Denham and the crew declined and returned to the ship. The chief didn't take the rejection lightly. Sometime after dark, a group of natives kidnapped Darrow from the ship and brought her back to Skull Island to become Kong's next sacrifice. Once the crew realized Ann had been taken captive, Denham, Driscoll, and others returned to rescue Darrow.

Unfortunately, it was too late for Ann. The natives had already offered her to Kong as a gift. Kong took her and stalked off into the jungle. Ann soon discovered she was not alone. Other creatures on the island began seeing her as their next snack, but they would have to go through Kong first. To save Ann, Kong fought off a Tyrannosaurus Rex and a Pterodactyl. While Kong battled for his life against these beasts, Driscoll located Ann. During the battle of monsters, Driscoll and Ann escaped Skull Island.

Once Ann and Driscoll returned to the ship, Denham captured Kong and brought him to New York. After the crew arrived in New York, King Kong and Ann were paired together for a spectacular show. In the 1933 version, Kong escaped, kidnapped Ann Darrow, and climbed the Empire State Building while battling airplanes. Kong died from bullet wounds and fell to his death. While standing next to Kong's body, Denham said, "It was beauty that killed the beast."

King Kong also appeared in other movies. In 1962, TOHO released *King Kong vs. Godzilla.* In 1986, King Kong came back for *King Kong Lives.* Since 1933, several King Kong remakes have been made, but true Kong fans still enjoy *King Kong Lives* and *King Kong vs. Godzilla.*

13

BIGFOOT

Bigfoot must be at least 100 years old and remains one of America's most elusive creatures. In fact, Bigfoot may be the only true monster in existence. Even with millions of web pages devoted to Bigfoot, no one can either prove or disprove its existence.

The Internet offers many opinions. The Animal Planet website lists their ten most popular Bigfoot sightings. They chose the Roger Patterson and Robert Gimlin film as their number one sighting. Some viewers consider the footage fake while others believe it proves Bigfoot's existence.

In 1967, Patterson and Gimlin captured an image of a large, hairy, ape-like creature wandering along Bluff Creek in Northern California. Patterson said his horse threw him after the creature first appeared. The beast turned, gazed into the camera, and then disappeared. Patterson's footage has become iconic. For more than forty years, brilliant minds alike have debated the film's authenticity.

Patterson died in 1972 of cancer. Before that, he never wavered from what he said in his film. Likewise, Gimlin has never altered his story from 1967. Even with modern technology, no one has ever completely discredited the Patterson-Gimlin film. Even before Patterson's film, people have reported Bigfoot sightings since the late 1800s. Animal Planet also mentioned a 1924 Bigfoot sighting by a Canadian man named Albert Ostman, who claimed a family of ape-like creatures kidnapped him and held him prisoner for several days.

He said the family included a male, female, and two youngsters. Ostman claimed the creatures communicated with grunts and other strange noises. Ostman said he escaped after the adult male ate his can of snuff and became ill. However, Ostman waited thirty years before mentioning the incident. He claimed he didn't tell anyone because he didn't want anyone to think he was crazy. Skeptics have since denounced the story, but without any further evidence, no one knows the truth.

In October of 2013, *The New York Daily News* presented the following headline: "Bigfoot Lives! Existence Backed by DNA, Video, Claim Sasquatch Genome Project Researchers." The researchers have footage of a furry creature in Kentucky sleeping in the woods. They managed to collect its hair and blood samples. Dr. Melba Ketchum, a genetics scientist, is leading the study to prove Bigfoot exists. As with other sightings, skeptics have denounced Ketchum's research.

One such critic is Professor Todd R. Disotell of the Department of Anthropology at New York University. He disputed Ketchum's work and shared his thoughts with ABCNews.com. He called Ketchum's research nonsense and a joke. "She is a laughing stock of people that are of a community that are already kind of wacko." He also said, "This was not reported in any scientific way whatsoever. It's complete junk science, and then she misinterprets it. She hasn't published in peer-reviewed papers on this stuff. I do not know how this got put together."

Professor Disotell says he has disproven the Yeti, Chupacabra, and Sasquatch. Thus, like other sightings, Ketchum's investigation hasn't uncovered the truth about this legendary creature either.

14

MEDUSA THE GORGON

Medusa the Gorgon had a face so hideous that no mortal could stare at it without turning into stone. Combine a menacing face and a head with snakes for hair, and you have one angry woman. Then, as if life couldn't get any worse, she had to defend herself constantly against warriors who wanted to kill her. A brave warrior named Perseus finally defeated Medusa in a fight to the death.

Although difficult to believe, Medusa was once a beautiful woman. Medusa, Stheno, and Euryale were the Gorgon sisters. Stheno and Euryale, Medusa's older sisters, were immortal while sister Medusa remained a mortal. When Athena punished Medusa, she made Medusa a mortal so that Perseus could kill her. Ovid, the Roman poet, wrote that Poseidon (God of the Sea) caused most of Medusa's troubles. Poseidon became relentless in his pursuit of Medusa. She had refused to make herself available because of her celibacy and devotion to the goddess Athena.

Poseidon discounted Medusa's piety and ravished her inside Athena's holy temple. Other stories suggest that Medusa claimed to be Greece's most beautiful woman, which angered Athena. Athena learned that Medusa and Poseidon had engaged in a sexual tryst inside Athena's sacred temple. Athena punished Medusa by transforming her from a beautiful maiden into a hideous beast. Anyone who gazed at her became stone. Medusa, while carrying Poseidon's off-spring inside her womb, left Greece in shame. Afterward, many warriors tried to kill Medusa because they knew her decapitated head was valuable—it could still turn enemies into stone. The only downside was they had to kill her first since she wasn't willingly donating her head.

Before Perseus, every warrior remained encased in stone while their sightless eyes gazed into eternity. These past failures did not deter King Polydectes of Seriphus. He dispatched a young warrior named Perseus to kill Medusa and bring back her head. To prepare for Medusa, Perseus received several exceptional weapons to destroy her.

Perseus had no intention of bringing a dagger to a sword fight. He received a significant arsenal of weapons from the gods. From Hephaestus, the blacksmith god, he received a powerful sword. He received a helmet of invisibility, gold winged sandals, and a shield with an inside mirror, which kept Perseus from looking into Medusa's eyes.

In Perseus, Medusa had met her match. The cunning, young warrior slipped into Medusa's lair and lopped off her head. After her death, she gave birth to Pegasus, the flying mount, and Chrysaor, the giant. Some stories claim they came from her womb while others say they rose from her blood. Again, this legend has many variations.

After Perseus had killed Medusa, her two sisters tried to extract their revenge by killing him. His helmet of invisibility and golden winged sandals helped him escape the vengeful sisters. Perseus presented Medusa's head to Athena, who placed it in the center of her shield as a trophy.

15

THE BOOGIEMAN

The Boogieman is an urban legend that has terrified children for centuries. So who or what is this strange creature? No one knows for sure because he exists in nearly every culture, which makes it difficult to comprehend his true origin.

The Boogieman has roots from North America to Asia. The Mother Nature Network describes the creature as one that will appear at a child's window with a sack for carrying off naughty children. For many years, parents have told their children to be obedient or the Boogieman will get them. Then Mom and Dad sit back and let little Johnny or Debbie's imagination fill in the blanks.

As with other monster legends, different countries have their variations. For instance, the Boogieman is also known as a Boggart, Bogeyman, Boogeyman, Bogyman, or a Bugge. Regardless, a child will want to avoid the Boogieman—even if it means obeying Mom and Dad.

Americans consider the Boogieman a frightening creature that just enjoys scaring naughty children. In other cultures, it kidnaps unruly children and will either imprison them or have them for dinner. No one knows what the Boogieman looks like or if it has a gender.

The Boogieman learns what a child fears most and uses the knowledge to become a child's worst nightmare. It only fears the light and will wait for darkness before approaching a victim. So it may be in a child's best interest to stay on Mom and Dad's good side, or the Boogieman is going to get them.

16

ORCS

Orcs are fantasy creatures made famous by J.R.R. Tolkien, author of *The Hobbit* and *Lord of the Rings* trilogy. Orcs are filthy creatures with a rotten odor. The Farlandworld.com website and the *Dungeons & Dragons Monstrous Manual* provide excellent details about these despicable creatures.

They vary in appearance because they have crossbred with humans, dwarves, and other species, which resulted in a creature called a half-Orc. Orcs are the size of an average human and have poor posture, a low forehead, and a pig-like snout. They also have sharp teeth used for ripping meat from bones, excellent night vision, wolf-like ears, and claw-like hands.

Orcs don't have an official language and may either stay underground or in a forest tribe. They communicate based on whatever language a tribe uses. Different Orc villages have their own dialects. The Orc lives to fight, destroy, and pilfer everything it can carry. They enjoy fighting so much that they aren't happy unless they are waging war against humans, elves, goblins, and dwarves—and if they cannot find something to fight about, they will attack other Orc tribes. They also worship their own deities. Orcs base their religious preferences on village customs.

17

COUNT DRACULA

Bram Stoker wrote *Dracula* during the 1800s. Many historians believe Stoker based Dracula on Vlad the Impaler (1431-1476), a heartless and cruel Romanian nobleman who tortured and killed people and animals. Although Stoker didn't invent the vampire legend, horror fans consider him responsible for the world's vampire craze.

Dracula begins with an English attorney named Jonathan Harker, who had a real estate transaction to complete with a nobleman named Count Dracula. Harker had agreed to meet Dracula at his castle in Transylvania. While traveling to Transylvania, peasants offered crucifixes and other religious items to Harker for protection against evil. He dismissed the peasant's fears and continued.

Harker found Count Dracula to be an educated and intelligent gentleman. Harker soon realized that he had become a prisoner and that Dracula was no mere mortal. He had unnatural superpowers and was likely from the pits of Hell. After three seductive female vampires tried to put the bite on Harker, Dracula intervened and saved him. He told the three sultry vampires that he was saving Harker for himself. Harker had seen enough and escaped the gloomy castle.

Enter Harker's fiancé, Wilhelmina "Mina" Murray, and her best friend, Lucy Westenra, who had received marriage proposals from

Doctor John Seward, Arthur Holmwood, and an American cowboy named Quincey Morris. Lucy accepted Holmwood's marriage proposal. After Mina visited Lucy in a town called Whitby, abnormal events occurred.

A Russian shipwreck with a missing crew was found. Inside the cargo space were fifty boxes of earth sent from Dracula's castle, which he had shipped to England. Shortly after, Lucy began to sleepwalk and was found in a cemetery with two bite marks on her neck. She started to waste away from a mysterious ailment. Dr. Seward summoned his mentor, Professor Van Helsing, to help diagnose Lucy. Though Van Helsing suspected vampires, he reserved his judgment. Lucy died after a wolf attacked her, but she didn't stay dead for long. After she died, Van Helsing learned that Lucy had become a vampire.

Originally, no one believed Van Helsing, but skepticism became a reality after rumors began about a beautiful woman who attacked children. When Van Helsing learned that this mysterious woman had bitten a child, he realized that Lucy was a vampire and must be destroyed. Arthur Holmwood slayed his former lover by plunging a stake into her heart while she slept. To prevent her from returning, she was beheaded, and her mouth was stuffed with garlic.

Afterward, Van Helsing, Morris, Harker, and a group of men vowed to destroy Count Dracula. The elusive Dracula found safety inside an asylum, where he planned to stalk Mina Harker and change her into a vampire by feeding on her blood. Once Harker and his group sterilized Dracula's earth, he returned to Transylvania. Dracula's pursuers followed him to Transylvania and placed religious items inside Dracula's castle. They also destroyed Dracula's three female vampire accomplices.

Finally, Harker and Morris cornered Dracula at his castle. During their final battle, Harker stabbed Dracula in the throat while a mortally wounded Morris plunged a Bowie knife into Dracula's heart, killing the vampire and turning him into dust.

Once Dracula died, Mina was freed from his curse. Unfortunately, Morris died while fighting Dracula. Stoker's story has led to several different film adaptations and spin-offs involving vampires, were-wolves, and other monsters listed in this book. Count Dracula will spend eternity striking fear into the hearts of anyone willing to read the novel or watch classic Dracula movies.

18

VAMPIRES

Vampire legends have existed for centuries. Many scholars and horror fans consider the Bram Stoker novel *Dracula* as the vampire authority. In addition, *Vampire: The Requiem for Dummies* separated vampire myths from legend. For instance, the book claimed that vampires feed on blood because their cursed bodies cry out for it. Vampires also have super strength and can transform into animals. Other myths are that vampires don't experience sexual feelings like humans. Furthermore, a wooden stake doesn't kill a vampire, it only immobilizes it. But the typical vampire will avoid sunlight, holy water, and other religious symbols.

Vampires attract moviegoers like no other monsters. Consider Stephanie Meyer's Twilight series, which involved a vampire named Edward Cullen, lovesick teenager Bella Swan, and Jacob, a werewolf who also loved Bella. Scores of teenagers happily paid millions for tickets to watch Twilight on the big screen.

The earliest vampire movies date back to the early 1900s. In 1909, *Vampire of the Coast* became the first accredited vampire movie. Another movie titled *The Vampire Trail* soon followed in 1910. In 1922, the Film Arts Guild released *Nosferatu*, a movie considered an unofficial version of Bram Stoker's *Dracula*.

According to The Live Science website, Matthew Beresford's book *From Demons to Dracula: The Creation of the Modern Vampire* says it's impossible to know when the vampire myth began. The vampire legend isn't traceable to one source, and the fascination of undead creatures that drink blood is global. Anne Rice wrote an excellent vampire series about a vampire named Lestat de Lioncourt. The vampire industry has made billions from movies, cartoons, and books. Alongside zombies, vampires have become an iconic and lucrative part of our culture.

19

WEREWOLVES

Werewolves are mystical beasts commonly known as lycanthropes: a mix of the Greek word Lykoi for wolf and Anthropos for man. The werewolf legend remains one of the world's oldest myths. The beast originates from European tales about a fierce, wolf-like creature that attacked, killed, and ravaged innocents.

Legend has it that werewolves can be detected in their human form. So be suspicious of anyone with curved fingernails and bushy eyebrows that meet at the nose bridge. This murderous creature has a distinctive walk, bristles under its tongue, and fur bulging from its wounds. If someone you know has these characteristics, he or she just might be a werewolf.

Early legends describe the werewolf as a wolf with human traits. The beast has a human's soulful eyes, no tail, and the ability to speak. Consider *Little Red Riding Hood*, a classic tale from Charles Perrault. In Perrault's story, a ravenous wolf devours the naïve Little Red Riding Hood and her grandmother.

Authors Jacob and Wilhelm Grimm replaced the original dark ending with one not so terrifying. In their version, a hunter cut the wolf open with an ax and rescued grandma and Little Red. However, the lesson remains the same—children should avoid strangers.

Most people familiar with this classic tale recognize the wolf as the antagonist, but he was not your average wolf. Little Red Riding Hood described the hungry wolf as if it were human. We know this because Red referred to the wolf's oversized eyes, arms, and legs. Who can forget the famous, "My Grandma, what big eyes you have" line? He had the capacity to think and speak the human language.

However, original European werewolf legends differ from Hollywood versions that starred actors David Naughton, Michael Landon, and Lon Chaney. Europeans believed that anyone who lived a wicked lifestyle was punished by becoming a werewolf. They believed people could become werewolves if they drank rainwater from a wolf's paw print, engaged in a Satanic ritual, or if they had angered God. Europeans believed werewolves could transform at will.

Then you have the Hollywood werewolf that can only change during a full moon and be killed by a silver bullet. Hollywood werewolves can also turn others into werewolves with a savage bite.

Werewolves also have super strength and are stronger than any individual human or wolf. They have heightened senses and can easily pick up the scent of their prey. Based on folklore, werewolves can only be cured by exorcism, medicine, or surgery.

Although the werewolf phenomenon has existed for centuries, no one knows how the myth began. Most likely, it started like other legends—as a result of superstition and fear. Consider two events from the 1500s. In 1521, a trio of killers named Philibert Montot, Pierre Burgot, and Michael Verdun were executed as the werewolves of Poligny. Another serial killer named Gilles Garnier was a recluse and a cannibal. A court tried him and charged him with being a lycanthrope and a witch after he confessed to killing at least four children.

He claimed a ghost had given him an ointment that enabled him to transform into a wolf. For his crimes, he was burned at the stake on January 18, 1573. Combine the horrific acts of serial killers and superstition and you have the making of an elaborate werewolf legend.

20

GREMLINS

Although gremlins do not have the notoriety of werewolves or zombies in the killing department, they have earned monster status. The word derives from the English word gremian, which means to vex. Although the little pests do not eat people or drink blood, they can still kill you. The gremlin is a mystical creature known for being a mischievous little miscreant that causes plane crashes by tampering with the plane's mechanics.

During the 1920s, Royal Air Force (RAF) pilots stationed overseas used the word gremlin to describe mechanical failures on their airplanes. In her book *The ATA: Women with Wings* (1938), pilot Pauline Gower described Scotland as gremlin country. Gower referred to gremlins as scissor-wielding creatures that cut the wires of biplanes. Also, avoid confusing the mysterious gremlin with a grotesque 1970 American Motors car called a Gremlin. Thankfully, the ugly little cars did not stay on the road for long after people decided against driving anything associated with a plane wreck.

If you want to know more about gremlins, I recommend the classic *Twilight Zone* episode starring actor William Shatner. The episode is based on a Richard Matheson story titled *Nightmare at 20,000 Feet*. Shatner plays Bob Wilson, a troubled man recovering from a nervous breakdown. He was on the road to recovery until he saw a strange creature clawing at one of the plane's wings. Once Wilson realized a gremlin was trying to destroy the plane, all hell broke loose. Wilson took action and saved his wife and the other passengers. Without revealing any further details, this timeless tale will give you an idea of why gremlins shouldn't be anywhere near our airplanes.

21

FRANKENSTEIN

Mary Shelley wrote *Frankenstein* during the early 1800s. The classic novel involved a creature with a grotesque face and a childish mentality. And like many children, the creature only wanted love and friendship. The unusual tale begins with Captain Robert Walton, who wrote to his sister about a creature that yearned for human compassion. Walton told his story from the frigid North Pole. After Walton's ship got stuck in ice at the North Pole, he listened to a macabre tale from a disturbed passenger named Victor Frankenstein.

The main characters involved Victor Frankenstein, his friend Henry Clerval, and Elizabeth Lavenza, Victor's adopted cousin and lifelong love. Alphonse Frankenstein (Victor's devoted father), rounds out the story. During college, Victor became obsessed with trying to reanimate dead tissue. By using tissue from corpses, he attempted to create a perfect human. Instead, Victor created a creature whose ugliness disgusted him. He then abandoned his creation and left it to fend for itself against humanity's cruelty and hatred.

Frankenstein's monster soon learned that beauty may be in the eye of the beholder, but it did not exist inside rotting flesh. In his misunderstood way, the creature tried to interact with humans.

The lonely monster awkwardly and unsuccessfully tried to find friendship and love. After experiencing rejection, the creature sought revenge against his creator for abandoning him. In his quest for revenge, Frankenstein's monster killed Elizabeth, Henry, and Victor's younger brother William. After the monster did away with William, his nanny, Justine Moritz, was falsely blamed for killing the youngster. The innocent nanny was hanged for the brutal killing after William's locket was found in her possession.

The monster located Victor and demanded a female companion. He told Victor, "My companion must be of the same species and have the same defects. This being you must create." Victor agreed to create a companion for the love starved creature, but after becoming wracked with guilt over the deaths attributed to his creation, he abandoned his attempt to create another monster.

Tragically, the deaths of Elizabeth, Henry, William, and Justine cause Alphonse to die from grief. Victor commits himself to destroying his monster. He pursues the monster to the North Pole for a final confrontation, which never occurred. Victor died and was found by his monster, who grieved over his creator's death. The creature destroyed itself and disappeared on a floating ice raft.

22

SHARKS

*J*aws is an American classic written by the late Peter Benchley. After the book enjoyed much success, Steven Spielberg directed the movie. What's terrifying about sharks is that they are real. They don't hide in caves, sleep during the daytime, or limit themselves to a special menu.

Sharks can become the same size as a pickup truck, but they aren't all dangerous. For instance, the Whale Shark and Basking Shark don't eat meat. But the Great White Shark and Tiger Shark aren't too picky. These monsters only live to eat and reproduce. They can also smell blood from miles away.

Near the end of WWII, the USS Indianapolis sank into the ocean after a Japanese submarine bombed the ship with torpedoes. It's estimated that 900 men survived the ship's sinking, but only 317 lived long enough to be rescued. Surviving sailors floated in shark infested waters for five days. Tiger sharks detected blood and moved in to feast on survivors. The incident is the worst naval disaster in American history.

Another reason that makes sharks monstrous is that no one knows how long they live, which make them appear immortal. And it's possible that sharks today may have lived alongside dinosaurs. Jaws was a Great White Shark that terrorized the fictitious Amity Island. Great Whites can grow from 15 to 20 feet long. Adult Great White sharks eat seals, smaller whales, and other sharks. Orcas, larger sharks, and man are their only natural enemies.

But when you weigh in at 5,000 pounds and have roughly 1,000 serrated teeth that can swallow a seal in its entirety, who will challenge you? Here's another tidbit to bite into: As large as a Great White Shark is, it isn't even the largest shark in the ocean. Whale sharks and Basking sharks can grow up to 40 feet. Thankfully, they don't eat meat or pose a threat to people. Whenever a shark attack occurs, it's often a Great White or a Tiger Shark; they are fearless monsters that will eat anything. Sharks deserve a spot in the archives of horror.

CONCLUSION

After reading this book, you now have a better understanding of the myths and legends that have terrified us for centuries. Consider the different monster books, movies, cartoons, clothing, and collectibles that constitute this billion-dollar industry.

We just cannot get enough of the gore and destruction brought on by our favorite monsters. The *Twilight* series took America by storm. And Stephanie Meyer has kept vampire hordes alive in our imaginations and our nightmares, which is where they need to be—not under our beds or hiding in our closets.

ABOUT THE AUTHOR

Marc Hoover writes a weekly column for the *Clermont County Sun*. He also writes local news and strange news stories for the *Examiner*. Marc loves zombies, vampires, ghost stories, and anything supernatural. Please visit his website: www.lifewithgrandpa.com and blog: www.wisegrandpa.com or email him at augustlake@fuse.net.

As a child, Marc Hoover fell in love with the movies that gave other children nightmares. Now, this lifelong fan of hair-raising stories and flesh-eating villains shares his monster expertise with the world.

Furthermore, Marc has earned his bachelor's and master's degrees from Indiana Wesleyan University. He currently lives in Ohio with his family. At night, while the rest of his household sleeps, Marc can be found savoring the works of George Romero and Richard Matheson.